LONGING TO HOLD

PRELUDE TO HARD TO LOVE

W WINTERS

Longing to Hold

W Winters

There's a moment when I forget he's not mine. This small spell of time, when I let my thoughts carry me away.

He holds me. He kisses me. He makes all of this better.

That moment when I'm his and everything is all right, is gone in an instant. It's quick and fleeting, moving so fast that it slips through my grasp. If I could catch it, I'd hold on to it forever.

I always thought this thing between us would

only ever be just that. A passing moment, a pleasant dream that helped lull me to sleep at night.

If I'd known what was to come, maybe I would have thought twice.

I couldn't have prepared for this.

Longing to Hold is a short prelude to the *Hard to Love* series.

LAURA

*O*ur eyes met for a fraction of a second. If that. It was in passing.

Him on one end of the cafeteria, and I at the other.

The clatter of trays hitting the tables in our high school cafeteria and the even louder chatter and laughter of everyone else faded into the background. The sounds weren't worthy of white noise. It all disappeared.

Despite being across the room I felt him then, his hands on me; I knew they'd be rough and possessive. His lips hit mine, hot and full of hunger, as if he'd been deprived of my touch. I could feel the hard cinder blocks scraping my back as he pushed me against the wall. I could hear the soft moans and heavy breathing I'd give to him the second his lips left mine and he stared deeply into my eyes.

Peering down at my tray, I can only hope my cheeks aren't as red as they are hot. It's hard to swallow, but I do. The perfectly red apple with no bruises or nicks holds absolutely no desire for me to eat any longer, but I bite into it again, not tasting a damn thing while I keep my head down.

I could look up to see if he noticed, but Seth King's table is full of other students, his crew as I've dubbed them, and mine is empty. One look and someone would see me staring at him; there's no one else here at my table to hide me or my sordid thoughts.

So I keep my head down and avoid the curious gazes of anyone watching. Just like I've been doing for weeks now. Ever since my dad died.

My throat's tight. It gets like that whenever I think of my father, and I nearly choke on the small piece of fruit in my mouth. Apple juice goes down the wrong way and I pretend that's why my eyes sting.

I'm dealing poorly with the loss and everything that happened just before it. I'm certain that's why everyone avoids me now.

It didn't used to be like this. I was never one of the popular girls, but I wasn't a pariah either. That must be it. I've become an emotional wreck, so now everyone keeps their distance. It seems fitting enough.

It's been weeks and only Cami talks to me since the car crash. Everyone else lets me be. I don't blame them. The simplest of questions or even a friendly wave—it's all met with a delayed response because my mind was elsewhere, or worse. I've cried out of nowhere more times than I can count. So now they leave me alone. I'm grateful, because it's embarrassing and I hate it. I hate how weak mourning has made me.

Everyone lets me be... everyone except for Seth King.

That has to be why I'm thinking of him like I am. Of all the thoughts of what he'd do to me.

He doesn't talk to me, not really. He doesn't do anything but walk me home. I didn't ask him to and at first I didn't want him there. I don't need an audience for my grieving and no one owes me anything, whether he knew my father or not. I told him just that, but it didn't deter him and to be honest, a piece of me was grateful that someone was there with me.

When the school bell rings and all my textbooks

are swept up and safely zippered into my backpack, I know he'll be there. Waiting for me as if he's supposed to be there. He doesn't even know me; not like that.

He doesn't tell me he'll be there, but I know when I walk out the double doors at the back of the gym, feeling the cool autumn air sweep my hair behind my neck, Seth will be standing at the edge of the parked cars. Which is directly in my path to walk home.

Seth's friends have been there as well lately, surrounding him when I get out.

I know the crowd of his friends, although I had no idea they even knew my name until recently. Everyone knows about them. They have a certain reputation.

They're the boys who are trouble. I know Derrick and all the things people say he does. Seth is their ringleader. That's a good way to put it.

Before I've even taken a step out of the building, I can hear Seth's voice. Most times, he glances through the people around him and sees me before anyone else does.

They usually disperse before I get there, but sometimes they're still talking. Especially Derrick; he doesn't seem to get the hint like the others do.

I'm not the kind of girl to allow a man to tell me to do anything. Certainly not Seth. I listened though. Not a piece of me wanted to be alone on the way home. All the evidence of how low my life had gotten was waiting for me. So I let him. He stands right at the entrance to the field, where anyone heading for the north side of town can walk right through a gap in the fence . Students like me.

I go to him; he walks me home. It's as simple as that.

But last week, his crew was talking and I didn't want to be a part of it. I didn't need Seth to walk me home and I definitely didn't need to wait around for him. I thought, I'm strong enough and I've had enough of Seth acting like my babysitter or whatever he thinks this is. I'm not one of them and I don't need to be a burden.

I walked around Derrick and Seth, not wanting to interrupt their conversation and not wanting to anticipate that he was waiting for me. Even though he'd been doing it every day I wanted to make it clear that I didn't assume it was going to last forever and, more importantly, that I didn't need him to. I didn't need his sympathy or whatever it was that convinced him he should be watching over me like he did.

After all, I barely know him. I know *of* him. It's different. His crew is older and they're all seniors. I'm only a sophomore.

Their fathers run the gang—*if that's what it's called?*—that my father was a part of.

I'm just the lonely girl Seth has to babysit, I think. Maybe his father told him to do it as a favor to my now dead father; I don't know. I don't care either.

So last week when I saw that their conversation wasn't coming to an end, I decided that if he's busy, I'll go about my business, refusing to be the inconvenience I knew I was.

Seth didn't like it, though. He didn't like me walking around them. He didn't like that I didn't wait.

I know that he didn't because of the way he yelled out my name. His voice was deep and full of irritation. The little hairs at the back of my neck stood up and it wasn't because of the chill that accompanies the end of October.

I couldn't even look over my shoulder at him. Instead I stood there for only a moment, frozen, watching the tall grass between the posts of the white fence waving in the breeze. And then my right foot moved, followed by my left. I kept my head down and continued forward.

He wasn't the boss of me and he still hadn't given me a reason as to why he was doing all of this. I still don't know for certain.

So I kept walking. None of them owe me anything. Regardless if they were close to my father or not. If they want to help because my dad worked with them, they can send money or something, I'm sure my grandma could use the help with the bills.

At least that's what I was thinking when I ignored him yelling after me.

Until his strong arm came from behind, wrapping around my lower belly. His forearm was solid against my hip and my back hit his chest.

"Wait for me, Babygirl," he whispered although his tone was rough and demanding. *Babygirl.* The name is probably inconsequential to him. I bet he calls a lot of girls that three-syllable nickname. It hit me hard though, like it meant more. It's like a memory you can't place. When it feels so familiar and comforting, but you don't know why. That's what his harshly spoken whisper, almost a reprimand, did to me. The girl I used to be wouldn't have tolerated it before. But that girl is long gone, and she took my will with her.

Seth's breath was warm on my neck. It traveled lower even through the cold. His hand slipped under my cardigan and lingered on my hip as his thumb brushed the exposed skin there. The layering tank top I had on beneath my sweater had ridden up when he moved to hold me.

It was maybe a third of minute, all of twenty achingly long seconds of him standing next to me, his heat enveloping me. I swear he runs hotter than everyone else.

I nodded, not trusting myself to speak and it's then that I noticed the other guys, most certainly Derrick, must be right behind me. I *felt* their presence. They followed too and they were close enough for me to hear although they whispered. The few students who walked around us stared. Great, I thought, now I've made a scene.

I heard Derrick's voice. That's what made me turn around to face all of them, something about having a good night, but he said my name with it. *Have a good night, Laura.* That's all it was. Derrick's first words to me were casual and seemingly innocuous.

I was going to say, *you too* like a normal person, even if it was weird that he'd speak to me. He never had before. But when I turned, Seth was there, too close, and with a look in his eyes I didn't care for.

8

Concern, disappointment, maybe something else as well when his gaze met mine.

It's been thirty-four days since the first time he walked me home. I count because I'm waiting for it to end.

Only twenty-two of those thirty-four days he actually walked me home. Twenty-two days of him by my side every step of the way after school. The weekends I've been alone to obsess over the change in events.

And seven days since that day I can't shake, when I disappointed him. When he called me *Babygirl*. It was last Thursday. And here I am, still wondering about it, replaying it and debating on where I should stand today if they're talking again. I won't walk off, because I don't want him to look at me like that again.

It's a foolish reason, but I know it to be true.

So all of this, this sexual tension between us, I know I've made it up in my mind. It's embarrassing and I hate it. If there was anything at all between us, he would have made that clear. He doesn't even speak to me apart from occasional niceties when we walk the fifteen minutes to my grandma's town-house. Nothing. And if I know anything at all about

Seth, it's that if he wanted me in any way, he would have been damn clear about that.

I'm just a girl who lost her father, and Seth is a boy who feels the need to make sure I'm okay because he knew my father. I'm sure that's all this is. But my mind wants it to be more.

Setting my apple down on the full tray of food I probably won't be able to stomach, I make a mistake and I look over at them. At the table of boys who are trouble at best, and dangerous at worst.

I just miss making eye contact with Seth's right-hand man, literally sitting to his right. Derrick's good looking; I get a glimpse of him first before cowardly averting my eyes and looking back down at my tray. He has the same dark brown hair as Seth but his is longer, swept to the side. He actually styles his hair. Seth's is shorter, but still long at the top. Long enough to barely grip maybe, but not much longer than that. Short enough not to have to style.

I've been doing that recently, I think with a touch of humor as I tap the plastic fork on the tray. I've been comparing every man I see to Seth. I always come to the same conclusion: they can't hold a candle to Seth.

It's his eyes though and his dominating aura around him that draw me to Seth. The piercing blue gaze, the broad shoulders and that strong jawline. Everything about him radiates power and sex appeal.

One more glance, just one, and I drink him in. Even though Seth's not overly muscular, he's toned and has enough of a defined outline of muscle that anyone who sees him knows he works out, or rather, that he could hurt them easily enough. It's what keeps his jaw sharp, I think. It's a clean line, severe like his gaze can be.

Apart from that, he's charming and classically handsome. When he smiles, *God when he smiles*, his pale blue eyes brighten, shining with humor, and his cheeks soften in a way that makes him more than approachable.

He doesn't smile much, though. Not recently.

I peek up, trying to disguise my curiosity as just coincidence that I'm looking his way again to see if he's smiling now.

My breath is stolen when our eyes lock and my heart does a weird thud; maybe it's pretending to be dead, just like I am. To no longer exist since he caught me in the act of daring to look his way.

Fuck, I'm shit at this. I've never been a good liar and I don't hide a damn thing well. I can't look away though, not when he's still staring back at me. I'm caught, literally and figuratively, stuck right where I am, feeling my skin tingle and my cheeks burn.

My heart's caught too.

It only beats again when he nods to the right, his head tilted, almost imperceptibly, motioning with it to come to him.

I can see myself doing it, walking over to him. I'd have to leave my tray behind though, because there isn't a place for me. There isn't room at his table. What would I do? Stand there like an imbecile waiting for his next demand? I'm foolish enough as it is.

What if when I got there, he hadn't called me over? What if all of it is all in my head?

I wonder if he knows what I'm thinking just by looking at me. I think he does because the corners of his mouth slip down as my lips part. As if I'd spoken the excuse. As if he could hear it from all the way over there.

"Hey," I hear a familiar voice say and the word comes with the clank of a tray hitting the cheap table. It jostles as Cami sits, her blond hair bouncing with tight curls as she tells me, "Sorry I'm late, fucking algebra." Picking up her apple she asks me, "You doing all right? You look a little flushed."

Emotions swarm up my chest and my cheeks

heat even more. "Fine," I answer her without looking in her eyes and refusing to look Seth's way again. "I'm fine."

I hate lying, but I'd rather do that than admit how irrefutably *not fine* I really am.

*D*errick shuts the door to his locker and it bangs louder than it should. I don't care; I keep the back of my head resting on the cool metal of the steel lockers and stare down the hall at room 4W with my hands in my pockets. I've never had a class in that room, but Laura has two of them every day in 4W.

"You really that pissed over her not coming to sit with you?" Derrick sounds exasperated and I turn back to him, not bothering to move even though the warning bell rings. The halls are mostly vacant, so I have plenty of time to get to the other wing of the school.

"She doesn't listen," I say, biting out the complaint lowly, although there's not much emotion in my comment. Laura Roth has a bad habit of doing what she wants, when she wants. And the bottom line is that she doesn't want me. Which is for the best, but I'll be damned if I don't want her.

"She's mourning," he reminds me and I give him a glare that would shut anyone else up.

"You don't have to remind me." I don't hide the anger in my tone as I make my way past him and down the corridor. I have nearly every class with Derrick. Thank fuck. I don't know how I'd get through the day without him there. I'm not a scholar, I'm not booksmart. With the life I lead, none of the curriculum taught within these walls means a damn thing.

"Get to class, you two," Miss Talbot calls out to a couple kissing in a corner. She's a nice enough lady, married and with kids of her own in college. Even her reprimand to those students sounds motherly. Her voice carries over to us along with her gaze and the moment she sees us, her lips slam shut. She visibly pales and looks to her right, clapping and telling someone else, apparently his name is Steven, that he can't be late again. She doesn't say shit to me or Derrick. No one does anymore.

Teachers like her are simply counting the days until we're gone and they don't have to deal with us.

I don't blame her. I don't blame any of them. I get it now, more than ever. Quite frankly, I've been counting down the days for years.

"I'm just saying," Derrick speaks beneath his breath, "she's not trying to be a problem, she's just out of it." My gaze narrows as I take in my friend. We're nearly the same height, but I'm still just a hair taller than him.

"Who said she was being a problem?"

"Cut it the fuck out. You know what I mean." The last student in front of us shuts her locker and practically runs off with two thick textbooks in her arms. Derrick gives her a tight smile that she returns with a blush and a quickened pace to get by us. "You're getting all pissed off because she didn't come over to sit at the table, but why would she? She makes it obvious she'd rather be alone." He continues, and soon the two of us are standing outside of our classroom sooner than I'd like. The door is still open and Derrick places his shoe against it deliberately, keeping it open. "You're letting her get to you. ... that's a problem whether you want to admit it or not."

I catch our English teacher's gaze as Mr. Chasting stares back at me before looking to his notebook and greeting the class. Not bothering to say a word to the two of us. He knows we'll come in, sit down, and deal with this last year just like he deals with us. Quietly, causing as few problems as possible and simply sliding by until we can walk across the stage at graduation and everyone can be done with this charade.

My response to him is firm. "She's not a problem and it's not a problem."

"You're right," he says, agreeing with me, catching me off guard. "You're the one with the problem. She's just a sweet girl you can't seem to leave alone."

"You know why."

"I do and I think it's fucked. My advice?" he offers although I don't want it. "Let it be," he hisses and I look over his shoulder to see a girl watching us from inside the class. I think her name is Sandra or maybe Susan. She's quick to avert her eyes and pretend like she wasn't trying to listen.

I barely react to Derrick's comments. I've heard it all before. I know how he feels and I don't give a shit. I can't stay away from her. I'm just walking her home. That's it. I owe her that at least.

"You've made your opinion known," I remind him, turning around to lean my back against the wall outside of the classroom. Seems like I need anything and everything to hold me up lately. It's fucking draining, dealing with all the shit that's gone down.

Derrick sighs audibly, as if I'm the worst thing he has to deal with. God knows that's not the case. Letting the door go, he stands beside me. The door shuts softly with a click and it's quiet for a moment before a resounding bell rings through the hall.

Now we're late. No one cares, though.

"I'm just saying," he continues, "she lost someone and maybe you should just leave her alone."

"Everyone lost someone." The words are lost in the vacant hall. "Including me," I add and turn to look Derrick in the eyes. Slipping his hands into his pockets, he nods solemnly. "I haven't forgotten," he answers.

"It's all different now, and if I want to deal with it this way, I need you to back me up." I feel tense and unsure, knowing everything has changed and I need Derrick here. I won't survive without him.

"I back you on everything, but you're supposed to trust me, and you know that means I won't be shy telling you when I think something's fucked."

A thin smirk graces my lips but it comes with a humorless huff of a laugh that sounds sick to my ears. "Everything's fucked." The past weekend was the hardest and the only bright light I had was knowing that come Monday, I'd have Laura to look out for again. Even if for only a moment.

I can hear him swallow thickly, and it's quiet for a minute.

"People mourn differently, yeah?" I ask him although it's rhetorical. They're his own words given back to him. Words he gave me when we stood over the ashes this past weekend.

His sneaker kicks against the cheap linoleum floors and I feel like a prick. "Sorry, I'm just being a dick now," I tell him and close my eyes, pushing down the pain of the brutal truth we've been hiding.

"No, you're right." He brushes it off but his voice is tight. "I like the way I handle it better."

"We should get to class," I speak when neither of us says anything for a long moment. His words stop me from moving more than an inch though.

"We're all dealing differently and when the news breaks, I know it'll be easier in some ways." I hate that he's talking about it at all. We made a pact not to say anything. A cold prick travels over my skin, starting at the back of my neck and working its way down slowly. My hands form into fists and I press the right one against the wall, letting my knuckles turn white.

The story is that our dads took off and we didn't

want to file a report. We don't need the police getting involved. Death is a part of this life. So is getting even.

I don't look at him when I speak. "It will get easier," I answer him, feeling my throat get so tight the words almost don't make it out. "This is what we signed up for. We knew what we were doing." I don't know who I'm trying to convince anymore.

"I know. And I'm here with you. Your right-hand man. I just feel like..." he trails off and scratches his jaw, staring down at his feet instead of meeting my gaze.

"Out with it," I say, biting out the words.

"Everyone lost someone and we're all dealing with it differently. But I don't get why you won't leave her alone."

"I'm just protecting her." The answer slips out easily enough. It's what I've told everyone.

Derrick scoffs. "Don't bullshit me."

"Fine," I answer him, subconsciously nodding as I tell him, "You're right. I want her and it's fucked. But I'm just being there for her, I'm not pushing anything."

He shakes his head slowly, his eyes pinned to mine. "You're waiting. You know it's going to happen. She wants you, you want her. It's going to happen and you're making sure it does."

"It will be her call if it does," I answer him, at peace with that decision.

"You can never have her. A lot of shit went down and more is coming. You really want to drag her into it?"

"She's already a part of it and you know it."

"Don't do this to her. You want to feel better, and I get it. But this? This is wrong." His conclusion is spoken hard and clear.

"Are you going to stop me?"

"No." His tone drops, as does his gaze. "I'll still be here. I won't stand in your way."

"Good. Drop it."

On some level I should feel relief that he's going to drop it, but I don't.

I don't think I can stop myself. And he's right; I don't deserve her after what I've done. But I can't help myself.

LAURA

*M*y shoulder's sore. I carried all my books around today rather than going to my locker and the damn strap has been digging into my shoulder. It hurts more than I try to show.

Secretly, as I make my way through the thinned crowd to the open double-doored exit, I hope Seth asks if he can carry my bag for me. I'm not a damsel in distress, but my pride is kind enough to acknowledge that it hurts. He always asks, and with my luck, I think: *today will be the day he doesn't ask and I'll have to ask him.*

I swallow the thought the moment the chilly November air hits me. Everyone scatters in front of me, but I stay where I am, my feet planted on the asphalt just outside the doors.

"Oh, sorry," I mumble when someone behind me brushes past and I realize I've been blocking the doorway.

A nervous heat ricochets through my body from my tiptoes all the way up to my ears, which turn red hot. I imagine they're about as red as my nose must be when I shiver and a cold gust of wind smacks me right across the face.

Unwilling to stand here any longer, growing colder by the second, I force myself forward toward the field.

My heart drops with each passing second. I have no right to be upset. This raw tightness in my throat can get the hell out of here. And it can take my insecure thoughts with it. One step. He's not mine. Therefore, there is no loss. Another step. I knew this wouldn't last.

Another step and I whirl around at the sound of my name.

Seth's face is flushed as he jogs to catch up to me. Tall and handsome, and literally running after me. *Blip*. My heart does a thing that feels like a mix between a sink and a flip.

"Couldn't wait for me?" he asks although it's

obviously rhetorical, stopping just in front of me. He's so close that his heat is immediate and with another gust of wind, I'm hit with his heady masculine scent.

"Sorry." My apology makes him noticeably flinch. With a tight smile, I shift my weight and adjust the strap of my bag.

"Let me get it." Seth doesn't ask, he tells me, and he reaches for my bag before I even have a chance to hand it over.

"Thank you." Relief is immediate.

"No problem." All sorts of emotions threaten to show themselves and instead, I bury them down. I shouldn't be this happy that he's here. We're still nothing. I'm just getting used to it. I look forward to it, even. I don't know what I'll do when he stops, but I don't want to think about that either.

"Are you still stalking me?" I manage to ask, even as the gratitude fills me.

"Of course," he answers with a cocky, asymmetric grin. "Technically," he adds and starts walking, his stride long enough to quickly put distance between us. He turns around to walk backward just as we get to the open gap in the fence. I'm faintly aware of the eyes on us, but I ignore them all. "Since I'm in front, you're the one who's stalking me," he teases with that handsome smile and my God, I laugh. It's genuine and loud enough for him to hear it.

"You wish," I tell him with a smile and feel the heat in my cheeks when he slows down so I can catch up. He made me jog a little to do it; maybe he wanted to make this chase even.

It will never be even though, I'm certain of that.

IT'S BEEN thirty-four days and it's then I decided I needed to write the little moments down. As the days blend together, the tension between us changes into something warmer, something closer. It's easier and lighter.

DAY 1: He told me he'd walk me home and that day I held his hand.

Day 24: He called me Babygirl. The first time he held me, even if it was only to stop me from leaving without him.

Day 36: He started meeting me outside my classroom and immediately takes my backpack without prompting when he sees me.

Day 45: It's too cold to walk, so Seth insists on driving me home. That's the day the news broke about his father. I hugged him and refused to let go for the longest time. And he let me, holding me back in return.

Day 46: My hand brushed against his more than once in the car and I swear I couldn't breathe because of it.

Day 50: I thought he was going to kiss me over the console. But he didn't.

FIFTY DAYS with Seth King so close. Fifty days of subtle touches and longing glances. It's not in my head. I know it's not. I just want him to kiss me. I'll be the one who loses in the end of whatever game he's playing. Because I'm already falling. I'm tired of fighting, though. I don't know how I can stop myself.

SETH

"You're a bad influence," Laura comments as she picks at the hole in her jeans. There's a broad, beautiful smile on her face though and a tempting tease in her tone. I fucking love it.

"Yeah," I answer her, grabbing another beer. "I know." The football game is on in the main room of The Club, so I invited her back here, to the back room.

Weekdays are no longer enough. I need her on the weekends too. Derrick warned me against mixing business with my personal life, but I can't tell the difference between the two anyway.

There's a pool table in front of us, and then there's only this amber brown leather sofa. Just those two pieces of furniture in the dimly lit back room, and just the two of us. Whenever I meet her gaze, the strong girl I know Laura to be is suddenly shy. Shy looks damn good on her. It only makes her look that much more fuckable.

"I don't really drink." The chilled beer in her hand moves to the other. Her thumb drags up the side of it, leaving a trail in the condensation against the cold glass.

"You have to at least try it," I say and brush my shoulder against hers, inching closer. Then I shrug as I add, "Or not," and take a swig of my own. Resting my elbows on my knees, I lean forward and tell her, looking over my shoulder, "You're right, I'm a bad influence. I'll drink it. I just didn't want to be rude and not offer you one." I want to ease her nerves, but I know part of the reason she's nervous is because she's waiting for me to make a move. She's getting bolder with every passing day. It'll happen soon; I know it. I'm fucking dying for it.

"'Kay," she answers me, and then takes a swig of her own. Her nose scrunches, but she swallows. Watching her lick her lips afterward makes my cock harden. I have to rip my gaze away and I focus on the cracked door as a roar of cheers drifts back to us.

28

"Someone did something good," she says quietly and I can hear her take another drink.

"Did you want to watch the game?" I question her, almost praying she says yes just so we're not alone back here. Everything is her call. But damn she's pushing me to give in with that innocent and tempting look in her eyes.

"As much as I like it out there, no, I want to play," she says and gestures to the pool table. Right. I drop my head, remembering that's why we're back here. It's not so I can fuck her on this sofa like I want to do. With Laura, the days feel like they're passing slower and slower until that moment she lets me walk her home. That short amount of time is a blur, leaving me wanting and waiting in agony until I can see her again. She's addictive. Her soft glances and gentle touches are my drug. *I want more.*

More than that, *she wants more.*

"What are we betting?"

"What do you want?" she asks me in return, the question deliberately seductive, and I have to swallow tightly, taking a long drink of my beer. I nearly finish the damn thing.

"How about if you win, you can pick where we go next Sunday," I offer her, knowing it's a win for me too.

"I like it here. I told you I was curious what it was like."

"I still can't believe you've never been here," I say before finishing the beer and stand, grabbing the rack to get the game started before all the blood in my head moves to my dick and I forget about the pool game again.

Laura follows my lead and says, "I don't see how you can't believe that... as I'm not twenty-one so I shouldn't be in a bar and this isn't exactly *my crew*."

"Crew," I repeat and lean back, grabbing the cue and lining it up. "You don't need to be in the *crew*," I emphasize the word, mocking the way she said it, "to hang out in here. Didn't you want a job? We need a new waitress and you don't have to be twenty-one for that."

She's quiet for a moment, not answering and I would give anything to know what she's thinking. Everyone knows The Club is our hangout and she's right, not everyone is welcome. It's only a bar, but it's where all the cash is funneled and laundered so all the dirty shit we do comes out clean in the books.

She finally relaxes her shoulders, letting the bottle sit on her knee to tell me, "I really love the atmosphere though. And the people... it's nice to be around here, I guess that's how I can put it."

"Well, I'm glad you came."

Just as I'm pulling back the pool cue, Laura calls out, "Uh, no. Ladies first." She pulls at the stick from behind me, and playfully nudges my shoulder. She teases, "And to think, I thought you were a gentleman."

I loosen my grip on the cue and when she has it fully in her grasp, I raise my hands, letting my gaze roam down her body. From the tight cream sweater to the faded pair of jeans with a hole in the knee, she looks utterly desirable. The cut on her sweater is lower than most of them. At school she's always hidden behind baggy sweatshirts. It doesn't escape my notice that she decided to wear a sexed-up version for today's venture. A not-date with yours truly.

"Whatever gave you the idea that I'm a gentleman... I take it back. You should know I'm practically a savage." My joke is rewarded with a sweet laugh and a complementary blush coloring her cheeks.

Laura rests the pool cue against the table so she can take another sip of beer before telling me, "I may have picked up on the savage part."

"You like the beer?" I ask her and she shrugs.

"So far I don't hate it."

I wait, taking my time for my next comment until she's lined up and pulled back.

"I heard you liked something else today," I start and watch her ass sway, her hips rocking as she teases the cue, letting the slim wood thread through her fingers as if she's a pro with it. I've got a full hard-on just from watching her, and I might be a bastard, because I'm not ashamed of it in the least.

"What's that?" she asks, squinting just so and ready to strike.

"Heard you told your girl Cami that you like my ass," I confess just as she pushes her weight forward, barely hitting the cue ball and bumping into the table as well. With her mouth hung open, although it comes with a smile she can't contain. A vibrant rose hue colors her chest all the way up to her cheeks. The balls smack against one another and only three break away, not giving her a damn thing.

"Speechless?" I question when she doesn't say anything, the butt of the pool stick hitting the floor as she holds it against her body.

My lips are on my beer, but my eyes stay on her as I drink.

"You're not a savage," she finally responds with more confidence than anything else, "you're an ass." She says it all with the most beautiful smile. I belt out a laugh, holding my hand out for the cue. She's resistant, pursing her lips, but gives in, passing me the stick.

Our fingers brush one another when she does. Electricity strikes me, coursing through my arm and then down my body. It's hot and the heat lingers long after she's sulked back to sofa, sitting on the armrest with her arms crossed against her chest. I want to feel that all the time. The way she makes me feel with such a simple touch.

"I don't remember saying a damn thing about your ass by the way," she says and shrugs. I make my hit quick, lining up an easy pocket shot. *Crack*. I move to the other side of the table, lining up another that should break up the rest of the balls. It's a more difficult setup, requiring a little more strength.

"Is that memory of yours selective?" I ask her and immediately pocket another ball. With the stick in my right hand, I round the table, daring to look back at her.

She's seething but the embarrassment, or anger, whatever's got her panties in a bunch, is mixed with desire that's been coming to the surface more and more with every passing day.

It's quiet until I pull back.

"You do have a nice ass," she mutters, and I look

over my shoulder to see her shrug, bringing her beer to her lips, her eyes focused on the ass in question.

"Glad I can give you a good view," I offer and just miss the next pocket.

Laura's giddiness is accompanied by a squeal of "my turn" and her quickly coming up behind me while her left arm brushes against my back and her fingers dance over mine. Every touch is deliberate, seductive, and I am drowning in all of it. I don't let go of the stick at once. When she tugs it, her eyes meet mine and the air sparks between us, getting hotter and lighter.

"My turn," she whispers, and I let go, not saying a word. I back up to the other end of the sofa, memorizing every curve of her body. She calls the side pocket and with a soft touch, the ball rolls lazily into the pocket. I have to wait until her back is to me to adjust myself. I'm uncomfortably hard, my cock pressing against the zipper of my jeans.

"We didn't come up with a bet," she reminds me when she misses her next. We trade places with little conversation, but the heat between us is there, and when she hands me the pool cue, she hesitates, forcing me to look into her eyes and see the smoldering heat that stirs in them.

"Right," I nod when she hits the cue ball, misses,

and makes her way back to the other end of the sofa, handing me the pool stick. I'm still standing where I was, watching her. Instead of going back to the table, I make my way to her, planting the stick down right in front of her, both of my hands around it as I ask her, "What is it that you want, Babygirl?"

Her beautiful blue eyes drop to my lips in a heartbeat. I know it's one heartbeat because my own pounds in my chest with lust and need.

"I can have anything?" she questions in a breathy whisper, slowly raising her gaze back to mine.

I lean in closer until my lips are only inches away from hers. "Anything you want." The tension sizzles between us.

Her chestnut hair falls in front of her, draping around her shoulders and I reach forward to tuck a lock behind her ear. I don't get the chance to though, because Laura's small hands reach up, grabbing on to mine. There's desperation in her touch, want and need swirling in a deadly concoction in her eyes.

"Seth," she says, trying to speak my name easily, but lust mingles with the single syllable. She closes her eyes, breathing in deeply, letting her chest rise and fall.

All I have to do is lean forward. That's it.

But the door whips open and Derrick's voice booms in, startling Laura.

She gasps and backs away, leaning deep into the sofa as I glare at Derrick.

"Oh shit, sorry," Derrick says and looks between the two of us. "I didn't mean to…"

"It's fine," I answer but my tone denotes that it's anything but fine. Clearing my throat, I ask him, "What is it?

"WE NEED YOU. SOME," he pauses and glances at Laura who looks down and away, like she's not listening as he continues, "information just came in."

I know exactly what he's referring to and it can't wait. Fucking figures.

"I have to go," I tell Laura rather than answering Derrick. "I'll drive you back."

"You don't have to," she answers sweetly, not at all bothered that our non-date ended as quickly as it began.

"It's not about what I have to do. Do you want me to?" I regret asking her that the moment the question slips out. Derrick's still here watching and I'm on edge waiting for her answer.

"Yes… please. I want you to."

Derrick butts in, responding to both of us. "We have to go that way anyway." He speaks to Laura this time. "So even if you said no, I'm sure Seth would have insisted." He's friendly toward her but I can see the warning when he looks back at me, the politeness when he looks at her. He still hasn't changed his mind.

I haven't changed my mind either.

* * *

"I hate your fucking guts," I mutter to Derrick and he only chuckles in response. Like all of this is some joke to him. The evening sky is already black, not a star in sight and with no streetlights in Laura's neighborhood, the only lights are from the windows lining the rows of townhouses.

"No you don't," he finally says, pulling out a cigarette and lighting it. "I was surprised you brought her to The Club. Didn't even know she was back there with you."

Nervousness pricks down my neck. I know exactly why he wouldn't think I'd bring her there.

"She wanted to do something this weekend. I offered to take her."

"Of all the places?" he questions, but doesn't say

anything else as I put the car into drive and make a right, driving back to the highway.

"You kiss her yet? Or was that your first and I completely cockblocked you?"

"The latter," I answer, tightening my grip on the wheel. My palms heat talking about this with him. He'd given up all the warnings for weeks now.

"So no kiss?" he asks like it's unbelievable.

"No kiss," I answer him, not bothering to hide my resentment toward him for interrupting us. I'm not just taking it slow. I'm letting her lead. Which is taking a longer time than I'd hoped. It's fucking torture but that's what I get.

"If that's not a sign, I don't know what is."

"What are you talking about?" *What sign?*

"That I just happen to walk back there and stop it. You're in too deep with her. And you know it."

"This again?" Anger forces my muscles to coil. "I told you, it's none of your business."

"It is my business, because you're my friend. My best friend. I'd give my life for you," he stresses in a pained statement.

"I'd do the same for you and you know that," I say and pause, making sure he accepts that as fact, "but she's not up for discussion."

"Could you even love her? Knowing that she doesn't know."

She'll never know. I've already decided that. She will never know the truth. It'll kill her. I won't allow that to happen. An intense wave of protectiveness jolts through me, leaving a cold sweat to cover every inch of my skin. Having to slow down at the stop sign, I look Derrick in the eyes and say, "There were only five of us in that room. They're all dead now except for you and me. She will never know."

"They could have told someone else. You don't know."

My head shakes in anger, denying what he's saying. No one else knows. They can't.

"I'm just saying, are you sure you want to go after her and not end this? It's not too late to walk away. She'll be all right, man. I'm telling you. She'll be fine if you walked away."

"I'm not walking away, Derrick. It'll be best for us if you never bring that shit up again."

He starts to apologize, but I cut him off, easing into traffic and aiming to end this conversation, "I made up my mind on how this is going to happen. If anything gets in my way, or threatens to get between me and Laura, there will be hell to pay. I want her, and I'm going to have her."

I know if she were to find out the truth, she'd hate me. I'll do everything I can to keep it a secret.

"She's going to fall for me," I speak out loud, wanting Derrick to know it, to accept it and get the hell over his reservations.

"Are you going to be able to give her that back?" he asks in a calm, even voice riddled with true concern. "Can you really fall for her, knowing what you did?"

If I were a better man, I'd keep her away because I don't know the answer to Derrick's question. I wouldn't dream every night for her to kiss me. He has it right. It's selfish of me to want her to be with me.

I'm not a better man. She makes me feel like one, though. That's why I can't stop.

I don't answer his question, and he doesn't bring it up again.

All I need is for Laura to kiss me. One kiss, and then I won't hold back a damn thing anymore.

BE PREPARED to be left breathless with this romantic suspense. Continue reading Seth and Laura's story, in Hard to Love, available now!

SNEAK PEEK AT MERCILESS

From *USA Today* bestselling author W Winters comes a heart-wrenching, edge-of-your-seat gripping, romantic suspense.

I should've known she would ruin me the moment I saw her.

Women like her are made to destroy men like me.

I couldn't resist her though.

Given to me to start a war; I was too eager to accept.

.　.　.

But I didn't know what she'd do to me. That she would change everything.

She sees through me in a way no one else ever has.

Her innocence and vulnerability make me weak for her and I hate it.

I know better than to give in to temptation.

A ruthless man doesn't let a soul close to him.

A cold-hearted man doesn't risk anything for anyone.

A powerful man with a beautiful woman at his mercy ... he doesn't fall for her.

CHAPTER 1

CARTER

War is coming.

It's something I've known for over two years.

Tick. Tock. Tick. Tock.

My jaw ticks in time with the skin over my knuckles turning white as my fist clenches tighter. The tension in my stiff shoulders rises and I have to remind myself to breathe in deep and let the strain of it all go away.

Tick. Tock. It's the only sound echoing off the walls of my office and with each passing of the pendulum the anger grows.

It's always like this before I go to a meet. This one in particular sends a thrill through my blood, the adrenaline pumping harder with each passing minute.

My gaze moves from the grandfather clock in my office to the shelves next to it and then beneath them to the box made of mahogany and steel. It's only three feet deep and tall and six feet long. It blends into the right wall of my office, surrounded by polished bookshelves that carry an aroma of old books.

I paid more than I should have simply to put on display. All any of this is a façade. People's perceptions are their reality. And so I paint the picture they need to see so I can use them as I see fit. The expensive books and paintings, polished furniture made of rare wood... All of it is bullshit.

Except for the box. The story that came with it will stay with me forever. In all of the years, it's the one of the few memories that I can pin point as a defining moment. The box never leaves me.

The words from the man who gave it to me are still as clear as is the memory of his pale green eyes, glassed over as he told me his story.

About how it kept him safe when he was a child. He told me how his mother had shoved him in it to protect him.

I swallow thickly, feeling my throat tighten and

the cord in my neck strain with the memory. He painted the picture so well.

He told me how he clung to his mother seeing how panicked she was. But he did as he was told, he stayed quiet in the safe box and could only listen while the men murdered his mother.

It was the story he gave me with the box he offered to barter for his life. And it reminded me of my own mother telling me goodbye before she passed.

Yes, his story was touching, but the defining moment is when I put the gun to his head and pulled the trigger regardless.

He tried to steal from me and then pay me with a box as if the money he laundered was a debt or a loan. William was good at stealing, at telling stories, but the fucker was a dumb prick.

I didn't get to where I am by playing nicely and being weak. That day I took the box that saved him as a reminder of who I was. Who I needed to be.

I made sure that box has been within my sight for every meeting I've had in this office. It's a reminder for me so I can stare at it in this god forsaken room as I make deal after deal with criminal after criminal and collect wealth and power like the dusty old books on these shelves.

It cost me a fortune to get this office exactly how I wanted. But if it were to burn down, I could buy it all over again.

Everything except for that box.

"You really think they're going through with it?" I hear Daniel, my brother, before I see him. The memories fade in an instant and my heart beat races faster than the tick tock of that fucking clock.

It takes a second for me to be conscious of my facial expression, to relax it and let go of the anger before I can raise my gaze to his.

"With the war and the deal? You think he'll go through with it?" he clarifies.

A small huff leaves me, accompanied by a smirk, "He wants this more than anything else," I answer him.

Daniel stalks into the room slowly, the heavy door to my office closing with a soft kick of his heel before he comes to stand across from me.

"And you're sure you want to be right in the middle of it?"

I lick my lower lip and stand from my desk, stretching as I do and turning my gaze to the window in my office. I can hear Daniel walking around the desk as I lean against it and cross my arms.

"We won't be in the middle of it. It'll be the two of them, our territory is close, but we can stay back."

"Bullshit. He wants you to fight with him and he's going to start this war tonight and you know it."

I nod slowly, the smell of Romano's cigars filling my lungs at the memory of him.

"There's still time to call it off," Daniel says and it makes my brow pinch and place a crease on my forehead. He can't be that naïve.

It's the first time I've really looked at him since he's been back. He spent years away. And every fucking day I fought for what we have. He's gone soft. Or maybe it's Addison that's turned him into the man standing in front of me.

"This war has to happen." My words are final and the tone is one not to be questioned. I may have grown this business on fear and anger. Each step forward followed by the hollow sound of a body dropping behind me, but that's not how it started. Y can't build an empire with blood stained hands and not expect death to follow you.

His dark eyes narrow as he pushes off the desk and moves closer to the window, his gaze flickering between me and the meticulously maintained garden stories below us.

"Are you sure you want to do this?" his voice is

low and I barely hear it. He doesn't look back at me and a chill flows down my arms and the back of my neck as I take in his stern expression.

It takes me back years ago. Back to when we had a choice and chose wrong.

When whether or not we wanted to go through with it meant something.

"There are men to the left of us," I tell him as I step forward and close the distance between us. "There are men to the right. There is no possible outcome where we don't pick a side."

He nods once and slides his thumb across the stubble on his chin before looking back at me. "And the girl?" he asks me, his eyes piercing into mine and reminding me that both of us survived, both of us fought, and each of us has a tragic path that led us to where we are today.

"Aria?" I dare to speak her name and the sound of my smooth voice seems to linger in the space between us. I don't wait for him to acknowledge me, or her rather.

"She has no choice." My voice tightens as I say the words.

Clearing my throat, I lean my palms against the window, feeling the frigid fall beneath my hands and leaning forward to see Addison beneath us, Daniel's

Addison. "What do you think they would have done to Addison if they'd succeeded in taking her?"

His jaw hardens but he doesn't answer my question. Instead he replies, "We don't know who it was who tried to take her from me."

I shrug as if it's semantics and not at all relevant. "Still. Women aren't meant to be touched, but they went for Addison first."

"That doesn't make it right," Daniel says with indignation in his tone.

"Isn't it better she come to us?" My head tilts as I question him and this time he takes a moment to respond.

"She's not one of us. Not like Addison and you know what Romano expects you to do with her."

"Yes, the daughter of the enemy…" My heart beats hard in my chest, and the steady rhythm reminds me of the ticking of the clock. "I know exactly what he wants me to do with her."

Merciless is available now.

Merciless World

A Kiss to Tell

Possessive

Merciless
Heartless
Breathless
Endless

All He'll Ever Be

A Kiss To Keep

A Single Glance
A Single Kiss
A Single Touch

Hard to Love
Desperate to Touch
Tempted to Kiss
Easy to Fall

Merciless World Spin Off

It's Our Secret

Standalone Novels:
Broken
Forget Me Not

Sins and Secrets Duets:
Imperfect (Imperfect Duet book 1)
Unforgiven (Imperfect Duet book 2)

Damaged (Damaged Duet book 1)
Scarred (Damaged Duet book 2)

Willow Winters
Standalone Novels:

Tell Me To Stay

Second Chance

Knocking Boots

Promise Me

Burned Promises

Collections

Don't Let Go

Deepen The Kiss

Valetti Crime Family Series:

Dirty Dom

His Hostage

Rough Touch

Cuffed Kiss

Bad Boy

Highest Bidder Series,
cowritten with Lauren Landish:

Bought

Sold

Owned

Given

Bad Boy Standalones,
cowritten with Lauren Landish:

Inked

Tempted

Mr. CEO

Forsaken, cowritten with B. B. Hamel

Happy reading and best wishes,

W Winters xx

ABOUT W WINTERS

Thank you so much for reading my romances. I'm just a stay at home mom and avid reader turned author and I couldn't be happier.
I hope you love my books as much as I do!

More by W Winters
www.willowwinterswrites.com/books/

Made in the USA
Middletown, DE
10 January 2024

47262362R00038